FRANKLY, FRANNIE

by AJ Stern • illustrated by Doreen Mulryan Marts

SCHOLASTIC INC.
New York Toronto London Auckland
Sydney Mexico City New Delhi Hong Kong

ISBN 978-0-545-29283-2

12 11 10 9 8 7 6 5 4 3 2 1   10 11 12 13 14 15/0

Printed in the U.S.A.   40

First Scholastic printing, September 2010

CHAPTER 1

"I have simply magnificent news!" Mrs. Pellington called from the front of the room.

We had just come back from gym class and we were still feeling run-aroundy, so Mrs. P. gave two long claps followed by three fast ones. This is our signal to clap back and concentrate.

I love clapping back songs. If there are jobs other than teaching where you get to song-clap, I want to work at one.

Mrs. P. always announces **"simply magnificent news"** on Thursdays. Mostly it's about school things like changes on the chore calendar or cleaning out the gerbil cage. But today, Elizabeth Sanders's dad was standing next to Mrs. P., which meant that maybe the news really *was* **simply magnificent**.

Elizabeth's dad is very important and interesting. **It is a scientific fact that he has his own radio show.** And if he has a radio show, then he must have an office. And if you don't already know this about me, **I love offices**.

If Mr. Sanders has an office, then he probably has an assistant. Which is the exact thing I told my parents I wanted for Christmas.

They're thinking about it.

Mrs. P. was so excited that she didn't wait long to blurt out, "Mr. Sanders has invited our class to visit his radio station on Election Day!" Then she covered her heart with both hands and gave Mr. Sanders big, blinky cartoon eyes.

Our whole class sucked in a fast gulp of happiness. Elizabeth acted like it was no big deal. But she only did this because Mr. Sanders is her dad. Secretly she was proud. I could see a really small smile on her face. I'm very smart about really small smiles.

Mr. Sanders's show is about news. My parents listen to *The Sandy Sanders Show* every morning. I am not supposed to say this in public, but my parents think that he is good at some things and not so good at others. A for instance of what I mean is that he's good at the news part, but not at the call-in part. Sometimes my parents slap their heads at his advice and say, "What on earth is he talking about?"

"Isn't this fabulous? Aren't we lucky?! We'll see firsthand how a radio station works," Mrs. P. said. Then she looked right at me and changed her face channel to strict.

"There will be special conditions for certain people."

That was when my whole body started to turn hot. This is because of what happened on the last class trip.

We went to the office of *Cambridge Magazine* and the office man let us all take turns in his swivel chair. We could swivel all we wanted, but we weren't to touch anything on his desk. But my dad says a messy desk is the sign of a messy mind. Maybe the office man didn't know this because his desk was very messy. When it was my turn in the chair, **I got a great idea**. And that idea was that when the office man's back was turned, I would surprise him by quickly organizing his papers.

But not everything went according to plan. When I reached over to straighten the papers, I knocked over a glass, which spilled water all over his desk. The office man was very upset. He kept squeezing his hands together saying the papers were "originals." My dad calls me an original, which is a good thing. So I didn't understand why the office man was so upset. Or why I got in such big trouble. Now I know. **Original means one of a kind.** Which is good if you're a person, but bad if you're wet paper.

"Does anyone have any questions for me?" Mr. Sanders asked.

My hand shot up so tall, I felt like I could have touched the ceiling without a ladder. Everyone else's hands shot up, too. When he chose me first, **I knew I had a really lucky arm.**

"Actually, Mr. Sanders, does a radio station have an office?" **Actually** is a really grown-up word and **I like to use grown-up words as oftenly as possible.**

"Yes, actually, we have a lot of offices."

See what I mean about **actually**?

"How many offices?" I asked.

"Everyone who works there has an office. And there are more than twenty people who work there."

More than *twenty* offices!? In one

place!? A veterinarian only had one office. A dentist sometimes had three. But twenty? They probably had a lot of staplers.

"But the most exciting office is the big one in the middle."

"Why?" I wanted to know.

"That's where all the action is. That's where all the disc jockeys work."

I raised my hand one more time.

"Yes, again?"

"How old do you have to be to work actually at a radio station?"

"Well, actually, some of our interns are as young as eighteen years old."

Eighteen? That was in **twenty-sixteen years!** I did not want to wait that long for a job.

At the end of the day, Mrs. P. gave us permission slips to take home.

But she pulled me aside. "Please ask your parents to come speak with me at school."

That is not such a good sentence. And that is a **scientific fact**.

CHAPTER

When I got home, I slammed the front door behind me so everyone would know I was there. At school they get mad when you do that.

"Frannie? That you?" my mom called from upstairs.

Frannie.

What kind of a name is that, anyway? It sounds too much like fanny, which is another word for butt. And butt is not such a nice word.

Frankly, **I** don't understand why kids can't just name themselves. (**Frankly! Now there's a good name!**)

"My name is *Frankly*!" I yelled, pulling open the refrigerator with both hands.

"Frankly, that you?" my mom called again. **I changed my name a lot.** My parents were used to it. Sometimes I added titles, like Doctor or Mrs., because they were really grown-up. "YES!" I shouted back, as I stuck my head in the refrigerator.

I pulled out some bread, a package of sliced turkey, mustard, and lettuce. **I am the only kid I know who likes mustard.**

Okay, here's a secret. **I don't *really* like mustard.** It's too spicy, but I like the *idea* of liking mustard. Every grown-up I know likes mustard and I want to do grown-up things.

I opened the lid on the mustard and sniffed. It made the inside of my nose crinkle. I quickly put the lid back on. I try to smell it as oftenly as I can. My dad says you can't be good at something without practice. So, I practice liking mustard. Ketchup isn't grown-up at all.

I held my sandwich in one hand, skimmed the wall with my other, and climbed the stairs to my parents' room on the second floor.

My mother was lying on the bed, reading the newspaper.

"Hi, button!" My mom's cheeks looked rosy. That's how they look when she's sick. My stomach flumped over.

I do not like when my mom is sick.

I felt tears welling up in my eyes. "You seemed okay when you drove me to school . . . And now you're in bed. Are you sick?"

It is a **scientific fact** that my mom drives me to school and that my best friend Elliott's mom drives me home. And Elliott, too, of course!

My mom smiled and scooted closer, wrapping me up in her arms. **I** love my mother **so so so so** much. She nuzzled my neck and kissed me all over my cheeks until her powdery smell rubbed off on me.

"No, Lovey Dove, I'm not sick."

I wanted to believe her, but she paused for too long before answering. **I'm** very smart about pauses. So maybe she wasn't telling the truth.

I put down my sandwich and ran to the bathroom as she called out, "Where are you going?"

"To get you some tissues."

When I returned, I held them to her nose and said, "Blow."

My mother laughed and gently lowered my arm. "I'm not sick, Lovey."

I ran back to the bathroom to get a thermometer and put it in her mouth, even though I didn't know how long to keep it there. I tapped my foot a couple times and looked at my wrist even though I did not wear a watch. Finally, it was boring, so I pulled the thermometer out of her mouth.

"Do you feel better now?" I asked.

"Lots," she said. And then, "May I sit up now?"

I picked my sandwich back up, shrugged, and with my mouth full, said, "I guess so."

"I know you think I'm sick, but I'm not. I just took a personal day."

"What's a personal day?"

"Sometimes people don't go to work because they're on vacation and sometimes people don't go to work because they're sick, but there's another kind of not going to work and that's called a personal day. When you take the day off because you have a lot of personal business to take care of."

This gave me an idea.

"Can I take a personal day?"

I could tell my mother thought this was hilarious because she laughed so hard, her eyes watered. Then she said, "Oh, Frannie, you are such a comedian." But I don't want to be a comedian. Comedians don't have offices.

"I'm not sure schools give out personal days," she said.

"Well, that's not very fair. Kids should be allowed the exact same things adults are allowed."

"You think adults have it pretty easy, don't you?"

"Yes, I do. Kids have it much harder." *Especially when they have to tell their parents Mrs. P. wants to talk with them.*

"It's not so easy for us, either, you know," said my mother.

I shrugged. I didn't believe her. She said things like this all the time just to make me feel better about not being older.

A while later the front door opened and we heard my dad singing along to his iPod. He's a really bad singer. Sometimes my mom and I cover our ears to joke with him.

I hopped off the bed and ran down the stairs.

"There's my Bird!" my dad called. I jumped up for a lift-hug. My dad is the only person who calls me Bird. It is a **scientific fact** that Bird is my middle name. **But please, do not tell anyone**.

"What's new with today?" he asked.

"I was mom's doctor and I fixed her, because I'm really good at that job. And I changed my name."

"What's your new name?" asked Dad.

I took a very long breath and then announced, "My name is now Frankly!" I said, looking down at all the mail in my father's hand. Opening mail was really grown-up.

My dad looked up at the ceiling for a minute, then back down at me.

"Frankly. I like it."

Then my mom came down and we all went into the kitchen and I helped make dinner. Some families say grace or a prayer before their meals, but not my family. My family says, **"To the Millers!"** because that is our last name.

After we said "To the Millers!" we talked about the news of the day. My parents like to talk about politics. I have very strong opinions about politics. And my opinions are that **politics are boring**.

"I have something to say."

"Well, we'd love to hear it," my dad said.

He and my mom both leaned back in their chairs. I had their full attention.

"My class is going to visit *The*

Sandy Sanders Show. At an actual real-life radio station."

"Uh-oh," was what my mother said.

My father inched his way back to the edge of his seat. "Hmmm . . . What did Mrs. Pellington have to say?"

That was the exact question I did not want to answer.

I answered it, anyway. "She wants to have a talk with you."

My dad folded his arms across his chest. "Yeah, she probably wants us to have a good long talk about the *Cambridge Magazine* trip and your curious hands."

"That was a long time ago. My hands are really different now!"

"Birdy, it was three weeks ago!"

"But I know better now! I won't touch anybody's desk. I promise."

I realized that I needed to be very serious. So I thought for a minute. The only way to show them how serious was to use my English accent. I spoke very slowly, just like Eliza Doolittle in *My Fair Lady*.

"It is a scien-tific faakt that I will nawt touch any-theng."

My parents looked at each other. They sent tricky smiles back and forth.

My dad said, "We'll see what rules Mrs. Pellington suggests."

My mom looked me directly in the eyeballs. "And you will have to follow them."

I flumped my hands to my side. I really hoped Mrs. P. was in a **simply magnificent** mood.

CHAPTER

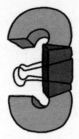

When I woke up the next morning, I had a hurricane of butterflies in my belly. That's what happens when I get nervous. My best friend, Elliott, gets moths. It's a **scientific fact** that butterflies are big and moths are small. He says he can feel a **machillion** wings in there and there's no way a **machillion** butterflies would be able to fit in his stomach. So they've got to be moths.

My mom was downstairs drinking

her coffee. I was trying to be very silent. **If my mother didn't hear me, maybe she'd forget about me and then maybe she would forget to take me to school.**

But before I even knew it, we were in the car. And before I even knew it again, we were already in the school parking lot. When we drove around to find a parking space, there were a lot of trucks. And coming out of the trucks were people carrying big booths. I guess I forgot about being silent because my mouth blurted out, "What are they doing?"

"They're carrying in the voting booths to get ready for next Tuesday."

"We're getting a new president?"

"No, it's time for a new mayor. Didn't Mrs. Pellington tell you?"

I shook my head no. But a little voice in my brain wasn't as sure. "Did she?" it asked.

"Chester Elementary is where the entire east side of town will vote for the mayor on Tuesday."

My mouth almost dropped off my face. My school was going to be one big voting office for the entire east side of town!

"That is actually really important," I said.

"It certainly is," said my mother.

Certainly is also very adult-sounding.

As my mom and I climbed up the stairs toward my classroom, I concentrated hard on sending a wish from my heart into her brain. The wish was: *I wish you would forget all about your meeting with Mrs. Pellington!* But it didn't work.

Mrs. Pellington was waiting at the top of the stairs. I thought if I stood there with both of them, it would stop them from talking about me, but that didn't work, either, because Mrs. Pellington said, "Frannie, why don't you go inside the classroom and give me and your mother one minute alone?"

I will actually tell you for a **scientific fact** that it was **absolutely**, **positively**, and **certainly** not just one minute. I know this because I counted. My entire class and I watched through the window on the classroom door as my mom and Mrs. Pellington talked. Then Elliott did armpit farts. All the kids laughed at this. I made my mouth laugh with the rest of the kids. I even acted out laugh noises, but my insides did not think it was funny at all.

I was too nervous about what my mom and Mrs. P. were **actually** saying to each other. I wanted to hear them but I couldn't.

I did hear someone shout, "Watch out, Millicent!" though. I turned around right as Millicent banged into Will. Millicent loved to read so much that anytime Mrs. P. turned her back, Millicent pulled out a book. Her hands were so fast that by the time Mrs. P. turned back again, Millicent's book was already hidden and she wore her "I'm paying the best attention of anyone" face.

When I turned back, my mom and Mrs. Pellington were shaking hands. Then my mom turned to wave to me and left.

As Mrs. Pellington walked back into the room, her face was very in-charge-ish. Almost like she was the mayor herself.

"Let's step outside the classroom and talk for a second," she whispered in my ear. I had a **maybe I'm not getting ANY presents for Christmas** feeling as I followed her out. What if I wasn't allowed to go on the trip? What if I had to sit in the classroom all by myself and wait **twenty-eighteen hours** for everyone to come back?

Mrs. Pellington cleared her throat. "Your mother and I talked and we decided that we will allow you to join the class on this trip."

I let out a sigh the size of the Grand Canyon.

"But . . ." added Mrs. P.

"I will be assigning special buddies for this trip."

And that's when I knew exactly where the no Christmas presents feeling was coming from.

CHAPTER

"Class, I will be assigning special buddies for this upcoming Tuesday's class trip," announced Mrs. P. when we got back to the classroom.

The best part about buddies is that we always get to choose our own. Elliott is always mine and I am always his. I knew how sad Elliott would be when he found out we would not be buddies this time. But before I could send him a note about it through my brainwaves,

Mrs. P. was already saying, "Millicent will be Frannie's buddy."

Millicent looked up and smiled at Mrs. P. in a very official way even though she secretly had a book on her lap and was not being official at all.

I could see all of Elliott's hopes pour through his body and drip onto the floor in a big disappointment puddle. If Millicent was truly a special buddy, then maybe on Tuesday she would let me switch her for Elliott.

Mrs. P. said she wanted to tell us a very good and funny story. I love stories and Mrs. P.'s are good because she tells us about what life was like in the olden times, when she was a kid.

I leaned forward to make sure not to miss anything. That was the exact moment that Elliott gave a note to

Sarah who gave it to Aaron who gave it to Elizabeth who gave it to Sasha who gave it to me. That was also the moment Millicent took her book back out and started reading again.

I love getting notes in class, even though it is against the law. I opened it up on my lap so Mrs. Pellington wouldn't see.

Elliott had drawn a picture of himself frowning. The word BUDDY was written on top and under the drawing his own name was crossed out. It gave me a sad feeling. I had to be very careful about sending a note because if I got caught, Mrs. P. might give me *two* "special buddies."

I drew a picture of myself and wrote, "Frankly Boredy Miller," which is a joke about being bored and also about my middle name. (Elliott is the only person who's not in my family who knows my middle name.) Then Elliott sent another note and I wrote him back again. Millicent squinched her face at me. She was getting the "Frannie's special buddy" job confused with the "Frannie's boss" job.

I looked right into Elliott's eyes and sent a note to his brain. It said, "We should probably pay attention now." I know he got it because we both turned to the front of the class to listen to Mrs. P.

". . . the election has been moved from our school to the local theater!" she said. I must have missed the end of her story because now she was talking about the election again.

CHAPTER

On Monday night, Mr. and Mrs. Wilson came over for dinner. They are my parents' bestest friends in the world. I like them because they talk to me like I am a real-life person, which is not the way all grown-ups talk to kids.

My mom let me wear her apron and my dad stapled together scrap paper so I could be the waitress and write down everyone's order on a pad. I went around the table, one by one, just like my favorite waitress, Betsy, does at Longfellows.

"May I take your order?" I asked Mr. Wilson.

"I will have the prime rib, rare, a pound of potatoes, a gravy boat, and yam soup."

"That will be one chicken pot pie and salad coming right up," which was **actually** what we were having for dinner.

"May I take your order?" I asked Mrs. Wilson.

"I will have thirteen slices of pizza, a frog leg sandwich in razzle-dazzle sauce, and asparagus lemonade."

"One chicken pot pie and salad coming right up."

Then I sat down and watched my

mom bring out the food that was too hot and too heavy for me to carry.

When we were finished with dinner, my dad let me be the busgirl. I'm a very good table clearer. Everyone thinks so and **that is not an opinion**.

Over dessert, they talked about who our mayor would be. Even though politics are boring, I felt very grown-up when they asked if I would vote for Frank Meloy.

"Does Frank Meloy carry a briefcase?" I asked.

"I think he does, yes," my dad answered.

"Then he's the person I would vote for," I announced.

"Because of the briefcase?" Mrs. Wilson asked.

"Not only. Also because both our names start with the same four letters. *And* because he carries a briefcase."

"Plus, he has a very good résumé," my mom said.

I looked up. "Résumé?"

"That's a list of all the jobs and schools a person has worked at and attended. You need one to get a job," said my mom.

"What's one look like?" I asked.

"I have some in my briefcase, actually," my dad said. "People applying to work at my office have sent me their résumés to look over. If you get me my briefcase, I'll show you one."

Before he even finished the sentence, I had his briefcase on his lap. He popped it open, pulled out

a small pile of papers, and handed
me the one on top. I held it very
carefully. I knew it was paper, but
still, it was very professional paper
and I did not want to make a crease.
Then I got a great idea.

"Can I borrow this?" I asked.

"If you're very careful," my dad said.

I looked right into his eyes. "I
will be very
careful."

"Then my
answer is yes."

After dinner I sat at my desk and pulled out my nicest paper. **If I brought my résumé with me to the radio station visit, then certainly I could get a job.** And if I brought business cards like the ones my dad has, they might want to give me a job even more. Business cards are for leaving your phone number and e-mail address with other business people. If you have a card, then nobody has to go looking for a pen and paper. My dad once showed me how he brings them to meetings and leaves them on a table all spread out like a fan.

I found a very serious pen that did not have an eraser and I looked at the résumé from my dad in order to write mine. **I carefully put down all of my jobs—Table Clearer, Temperature Taker, Mustard Sniffer.** When I was done, I put it in my dad's old briefcase, which I found in the basement, along with some other workerish things like paper clips, a legal pad, an old cell phone, and an old pair of glasses with the lenses missing. And when I finished that, I cut up an empty Kleenex box and made business cards that said:

Mrs. Frankly B. Miller
Radio Show Host
914-555-1819
MrsFranklyB@Millers.com

I put those in my briefcase as well. I was so excited, I almost couldn't fall asleep that night. I knew that if they liked my résumé and business card at the radio station, there was a chance they'd give me a job!

CHAPTER

Even though Millicent was also my special buddy for the bus, the ride to the radio station was still fun. Everyone was so **excitified** that we filled the air up with extra loud chattiness. I could tell that Mrs. P. was happy, too. **A for instance of what I mean** is that she led us in a round of my favorite clapping song!

Double, double this this

Double, double that that
Double this, double that
Double, double this that

Before my clapping hands even knew
it, we were at the most professional
radio station building I'd ever seen. On
the street we lined up with our special
buddies and then, when Mrs. Pellington
said we could, we **roundy rounded** inside
the building using a revolving door!
Inside, there were lots of people rushing
around importantly. Elliott's mouth
dropped off his entire face. He pointed.

"You. Are. Not. Going. To. Believe.
This." I followed his finger. There was a
little store with at least a **hundredteen**
shelves of candy and gum! **I had, had,
had to work there.** I never knew
that work buildings had places to buy

candy. For breakfast! Even Millicent looked up from her book to see all the deliciousity. And Elizabeth seemed really excited, too. Her smile wasn't nearly as big as mine or Elliott's, but I'm really smart about amounts of excitement, so I knew she was happy. But then, you will not even believe the rest. It is a **scientific fact** that:

1. There were turnstiles **INSIDE** the building
2. We had to get our picture taken
3. The picture was put on a special, real-life professional pass
4. That
5. We
6. Got
7. To
8. KEEP!

I almost hyperventilated from the excitement of it all. I held on really tightly to the pass even though it was fastened to a necklace made of tiny, little silver balls. I kept looking at the pass and every time I saw my face on it, my heart started thumping extra hard.

Then we got in a line and a very nice lady handed out white stickers for name tags. We took turns waiting for the magic marker, which gave me time to think. When it was my turn, I very carefully wrote my name in the **neatest** letters my hand could make: MRS. FRANKLY B. MILLER. When it was Millicent's turn, Elliott tapped her on the shoulder to get her to stop reading. His tap said, "I wish *I* was Frannie's buddy."

Then we went through the turnstiles in the lobby to a bank of elevators. There were eight elevators there. Just like in the Chester Mall! When I looked over at Elliott, he sent me big-buggy eyes which meant he was also hyperventilating.

When we got into the elevator, Mrs. Pellington pressed sixteen. And that's when I knew just how lucky a day this would be. My **very luckiest** number in the universe is seven, and one plus six equals seven. When the doors opened, we could hear *The Sandy Sanders Show* over the loudspeaker. There were a **machillion** framed posters on the wall and one of them read: THE SANDY SANDERS SHOW. I imagined another poster right next to it that read: THE FRANKLY B. MILLER SHOW.

When Mrs. Pellington told us to
hold hands with our buddy, Elliott
looked back at me with sad eyes.
Millicent took my hand, but I could
tell she wished it were a book.

A lady who sat behind a big,
round desk pointed us to a waiting
room with lots of radio magazines.
There was a bowl of mints on
the table, which Mrs. Pellington
quickly took away. That's when
I pulled out three business cards
from my briefcase and fanned
them out right where the candy
had been. Elliott looked very
impressed. So did other kids in my
class. Drew asked me if he could
have one. But he didn't have a job
to give me so I had to say no.

When Mrs. P. came back, she gave the longest, most **boringest** speech in the entire universe. And the worst part was that she looked at me the whole time!

As she talked, I realized that I had to go to the bathroom. I wanted to hold it in as long as possible because that felt like something an adult would do. But after a little while, I was not so sure how adults did this because it was getting very hard to sit still. **I jittered** my knees. **I crossed** my legs. **I stood** up. I **sat** back down. I stood up again. Finally, Mrs. Pellington said, "Frannie, what on earth is going on with you?"

Now was my chance to tell her, but I was too embarrassed to say it in front of my whole class.

"My legs are very excited," I said.

"Well, sit back down, please. You can stand when the tour guide gets here, which should be any minute."

I sat back down and realized right then that I was not adult in the holding in way. I needed to get Mrs. Pellington alone so I could tell her this in a whisper.

CHAPTER

The tour guide's hair was dyed purple but just at her bangs. I wondered if her parents were really mad about that. She was very bouncy. I think she was even more excited than we were. I guess Elizabeth already forgot the part about not being rude because before she could stop it, she blurted, "Where's my dad?"

"He's doing his show, silly! And when he's done at ten o'clock, he will show you all the inside of the actual radio studio. And you will each get the chance to sit in the host's chair."

That's where we all **ooohed** and **ahhhed**.

"Okay, class, let's get in line," Mrs. Pellington said. I took Millicent's hand with my left one and held my briefcase with my right. We followed the tour guide down the hallway. The tour guide's name was Tuesday. I had never heard a person named after a day of the week. This was very interesting to me, especially because Tuesday was not actually the best day of the week.

Off the long hallway were some of the twenty offices that Mr. Sanders had told us about. I tried to peek and see what radio offices looked like, but we were walking too fast. All I saw was a tray with a stack of paper in it. When I got home, I had to remember to put a tray with a stack of paper on my desk.

Finally we stood in front of a huge glass window and inside we saw Mr. Sanders wearing headphones and talking and laughing into a microphone.

There was a machine in front of him with a lot of buttons and Mr. Sanders pressed some but not others. He looked really professional with headphones on. It was the most gigantic room ever. There was a big, black sign and in red neon it yelled, "ON AIR." When I got home I also had to remember to make an ON AIR sign for my bedroom.

The door to the studio was really thick and had a sign that read: DO NOT

OPEN THIS DOOR! There were so many things I needed to remember but I was in pain because I **REALLY, REALLY** had to go to the bathroom.

"We'll come back when the show is over and then we'll go inside and Mr. Sanders will give everyone a chance in front of the microphone," Tuesday said. "Now, I want to give you a tour of the offices."

How would I pay attention to all the offices if the only thing I could think about was how badly I had to go to the bathroom?

Everyone started to follow Tuesday down the hall and I raised my arm and Mrs. Pellington called on me. I waved my hand at her so she'd come over to me and I could whisper.

When she bent down, I said very

quietly, "I *really* have to go to the bathroom." She gave me a bothered look, but then called Tuesday over who said the bathroom was just right down the hall.

Millicent and I ran down the hall with my briefcase slapping against my leg and when I opened the bathroom door, Millicent banged into it. Do you want to know why? Because she was reading! While she was running!

"Millicent!" I scolded. "You are not paying attention!"

"I am *too* paying attention!" she said. "But in the book, Jackie just told Joanna a secret, but Joanna got the secret wrong!" Secrets interested me. Maybe Millicent could tell me the secret later when we weren't rushing.

The bathroom was the biggest I'd ever seen. It was as big as the radio studio! There was an **actual** real chair, like the kind we had at home in our living room! And there was a basket of makeup that was free! And another basket with candy! This made Millicent put down her book. Elliott was not going to believe this.

I went to the bathroom as fast as is **scientifically possible** and then Millicent and **I** went to catch up with our class. But when we came out of the bathroom, our class wasn't standing where it stood before. We didn't see anyone anywhere. I looked at Millicent who looked just as confused as I was.

"What should we do?" she asked.

"I don't know!"

She grabbed my hand and we ran down the hall. As we neared the studio door, I noticed that it was open and no one was inside hosting the show!

This was not a good sign and I knew it. I looked at the clock and it said 9:45 AM. That meant there were only fifteen minutes left of the show. Which meant it was the end of the show, which meant it was the call-in part of the show—the part where Mr. Sanders gave advice. Maybe my parents weren't the only ones who thought he wasn't good at this part of the show. Maybe someone told him and he got upset and left? What if he was crying by himself in his office? If that was the case, then who would do the advice part? **I know that I give really good advice because**

sometimes my dad says to me,
"Good advice, Bird!"

I felt sad Mr. Sanders was so upset
that he had to leave his own show, but
I also knew the saying "The show
must go on!" It couldn't go on without
Mr. Sanders, though. Unless . . .
Unless . . .

I looked at Millicent who looked
stumpified.

"We have to go in there to help Mr.
Sanders," I said.

"We're not allowed!" she protested.

"But it's an emergency!" I cried.
Mr. Sanders was going to really
appreciate this. He'd probably give
me my own radio show.

I grabbed Millicent's hand and ran
inside the studio. She closed the door
behind us and looked really worried.

"We're going to get in trouble," she said.

I ran over to Mr. Sanders's chair and put my briefcase on the table. Then I clicked it wide open and took out the things that made me look **workerish**. I put the glasses with no lenses on my face, but they were too big and fell off. Then I sat in Mr. Sanders's chair (which was still warm) and put on his headphones. Those slid right off my head, too, but I adjusted them so they'd fit better.

When I looked over at Millicent, she had forgotten about getting in trouble because she was on the floor, reading the last pages of her book. Just then I heard a smacking sound. There was a man behind a glass window and he had headphones on, too! He was banging on the glass and pointing. I gave a big smile because I knew he was trying to thank me for **saving the day**.

Just then the phone rang and I looked at Millicent.

"Should I answer it?"

Without looking up, she said, "Well, it is the advice part of the show."

She was right. It *was* the advice part of the show. I *had* to press the blinking light. I *had* to answer the phone. As I reached toward the blinking light, there was even more banging on the window. Now, a different man was making signals with his hands. He looked like an umpire in a baseball game. And since my dad watches baseball games, I know what the signals mean. When the umpire shakes his head no while moving a hand across his neck, it means, "You're out!" That was what the man was doing now. He was saying that

Mr. Sanders was "out." Which meant he was in big trouble. A different man was making the "safe" sign, which meant I was safe to answer the phone.

I pressed the red blinking button. Then some people in the booth slapped their palms against their foreheads. Another guy put his head down on the table. They were really impressed.

"Hello?"

I heard my *hello* fill the headphones. I was a radio host! I was saving the day! I was **ON AIR**! It was the best feeling in the entire universe. **And that is not an opinion.**

CHAPTER

Right when I answered the phone, I saw Mrs. Pellington and my entire class race down the hall to watch me. **I felt so much pride-itity that they were running back to see me.** They must not have wanted to miss a centimeter of my show!

When they reached the window outside the DJ booth, Mrs. Pellington slapped her hands against the window, too. She did it over and over like people stamp their feet at games when their team is winning. **I felt so proud of myself.**

"Hello?" I said again.

I turned to smile at my class just then. The first face I saw was Elliott's. He breathed on the glass window and with his finger wrote: "WOW!" **I was WOWING** everyone, **even Elliott!** And he is very hard to wow. Then Mrs. Pellington tried so hard to come into the studio to be part of the action, but she couldn't get the door open. She motioned to Millicent, who was reading. Millicent was going to get in BIG trouble now because she was reading and not paying attention!

A woman's voice said, "Hi. Is this *The Sandy Sanders Show*?"

"Yes," I answered proudly.

"But you're not Mr. Sanders."

"No, I'm Mrs. Frankly B. Miller. I'm taking over for Mr. Sanders. Do you have a question?"

"Ahhhh . . . okay. Well, Mrs. Miller, I do have a question and I'm hoping you can help me with it."

That was my chance to say the thing Mr. Sanders always said: "I'll give it my best shot."

I was really good at this!

"My husband and I are having a little disagreement. He says the polls at Chester Elementary are open until 8 PM tonight, but I think they close at 5 PM like the post office. Who's right?"

I could not believe my luck! Someone was asking me the most adult question I've ever been asked in my entire life! I wanted to memorize the feeling and tell it to my parents and their parents and their parents' parents and everyone's parents! I looked over at Mrs. Pellington whom I imagined was thinking how much I'd grown up since the *Cambridge Magazine* visit. Mrs. Pellington was holding one hand to her chest and the other to her open mouth. **It is a scientific fact** that people do that when they are really happy that someone is saving the day.

It was a good thing that I was also good at doing two things at once. **I** was very good at daydreaming and listening at the same time, which is how I remembered that Mrs. Pellington said that thing about how the elections wouldn't be at our school anymore.

"Well, actually, you are both wrong," I said. I couldn't believe my own ears! **I** was telling one adult that she and *another* adult were wrong and **I** wasn't even getting in trouble for it!

"What do you mean?" the woman asked.

"The election moved. It's not even *at* Chester Elementary School. It's somewhere else."

"It's somewhere else? Well, where?"

I squinched my brain to try and remember where Mrs. P. said all the elections would be. And then, I remembered!

"The local theater!" I said.

"You mean the Morristown Playhouse?"

"Yes! The Morristown Playhouse. That's the local theater."

"But that's in Morristown!"

"Well, they don't have voting in schools anymore. It's a new rule. You can only vote in local theaters, so everyone has to go to the Morristown Playhouse if they want to vote."

The strangest thing is that when I

said these words, they didn't make a lot of sense, not even to my own two ears. But I was saying exactly the words Mrs. Pellington said, so they had to be true. Then an even stranger thing happened. I heard voices talking in my headphones and they weren't my voices!

"Bob, call Victoria. Get her down here. Now!" said one man's voice.

"Little girl? Little girl? Can you hear me? Get off the mic. Get off the mic," said a woman's voice.

A different man said, "Steve, Victoria doesn't have the master key. Get Sandy, he's got a copy. Or get a janitor!"

I did not understand the code words of radio station people. But I would make sure to ask them what everything meant later. Now there were several people at the door, trying to get it open! People were trying all different keys. That's how much they wanted to come and watch me!

I looked over at Millicent with the **biggest grin** that my face ever invented. And that was the exact moment she reached the last page in her book and looked up. Mrs. P. motioned for her to open the door.

"It's locked," Millicent called, confused.

When I looked over at the door, I saw the janitors searching their gigantic key chains for the right key. Even they wanted to personally congratulate me. And then Mr. Sanders came back! Sometimes after being upset with my parents, I come downstairs to let them know I'm feeling better. I guess that's what Mr. Sanders was doing now. I wondered if it was a good time to give him my résumé.

Just then, I looked down and not just one line was blinking red for me, but **ALL THE LINES WERE BLINKING RED FOR ME**! I felt more important than a doctor!

As I went to answer another call, a high-pitched shriek came through the headphones. It was so loud that it hurt and I had to throw the headphones off. When I put the headphones back on, there was no sound. I thought for at least one centimeter of a second that I was deaf. I tried talking into the microphone and was very relieved when I heard my own voice. What

I did not hear, though, was my own voice in the headphones like I did before. The microphone didn't make my voice sound louder than it was. That's when I got a very bad feeling.

I wished and hoped for one thing. And that was that I didn't break the radio station.

CHAPTER

At just the instance that I
wondered whether I broke the radio
station, the janitors opened the door,
but the only person to rush in was Mr.
Sanders. He ran toward me. I thought
he was going to shake my hand or
hug me or ask for my business card,
but he didn't do any of those things.
What he did, actually, was lift me up
out of his seat and put me down right
next to Millicent! Then he sat where

I was sitting and put the headphones back on his head. He started pushing buttons and pulling at levers. He didn't seem happy like I thought he'd be. I decided to wait and give him my résumé later.

Then Mrs. Pellington came rushing in saying, "I'm sorry, I'm sorry, I'm sorry!" What was she apologizing for? There was a lot more yelling back and forth. Mr. Sanders was yelling about circuits to the engineers and the engineers were yelling about "kids today."

And then Tuesday, the tour guide, came rushing in with a very red face. She told us to hurry up and get out.

We were all so confused. We had only been there for forty-five minutes and we were supposed to be there for three entire hours! Drew started to complain that he didn't get to see as much as I saw. Then everyone (except Elliott, Elizabeth, and Millicent) complained that they didn't get to see anything, either! Mrs. Pellington was grabbing at her hands and looked more worried than I'd ever seen her. We didn't know why in the world we were leaving.

Going down the elevator wasn't as exciting as coming up. Passing all the important people and going through the turnstiles and saying good-bye to security wasn't as much fun. Instead, everything felt bad, like I had done something really wrong. Did I just have another *Cambridge Magazine* accident? No, it couldn't be that. I didn't spill anything on any originals. I didn't even see any originals to spill on. I was just trying to help Mr. Sanders.

We all stood crowded on the street, but our school bus wasn't there. "We're not supposed to be finished for another two hours!" said Mrs. Pellington, who sounded very worried. Then she started to dial her cell phone like crazy.

All my classmates surrounded me to ask a **machillion** questions about what it felt like to be on the radio. There was no way I could **actually** answer all of them. That's how many there were. I felt like a movie star. It was only when I realized their questions were getting hard to hear that I began to notice all the cars honking. The honking was really bad, and when I looked up, I saw the hugest traffic jam in the existence of the planet. Drivers were getting out of their cars and yelling at one another. Other drivers were hanging out of their windows waving their fists in the air. I wondered if something very bad had happened. I really hoped not.

Mrs. Pellington was talking to the people who worked in the lobby and all they did was shrug at her. Even when she said in her very worried voice, "We're going to be stuck here forever!"

But we weren't stuck there forever. Even though it took a long time, a bus finally came to pick us up. There was so much traffic that we didn't move a **centimeter** for a really long time. In that really long time, Mrs. P. said she was too angry to speak, and that we would discuss this "**fiasco**" at our class meeting tomorrow.

CHAPTER

The second I walked into our house, my parents had their "You're in big trouble, young lady" faces on. I don't know how they already knew about the radio station visit.

I'd never seen my dad so burning mad before in all of my life. He had his arms crossed and my mom had her hands on her hips. I didn't know what to do, so I just stood there, holding my briefcase, waiting for something to happen.

"You promised us you'd be on your best behavior!"

"I was!"

"Taking over a radio show was your best behavior?"

"It was an emergency! Mr. Sanders was in trouble!"

"It was *not* an emergency and Mr. Sanders was *not* in trouble!"

"He was, too, in trouble! He left the studio . . ."

"Mr. Sanders left the studio because he went to the bathroom!"

Huh?

The bathroom?

I hadn't even thought of that.

I had a very big trouble feeling.

"You were not thinking, Frances."

My mom Frances-ed me. I was in even bigger trouble than I thought.

"We are extremely upset with you," my father said as he began to pace.

"You caused absolute mayhem, not just for the radio station, but for the entire town!" my mother cried.

Huh? The entire town? **How in the whole wide world of America could that have been true?**

"There are still traffic jams out there," my father said.

I did not know what the traffic jams had to do with anything. Maybe my parents were so mad that they decided to blame everything bad that ever happened on me!

"Do you know how long it took me to get home?" my mother said, with her voice raised.

"How long?" I asked, but when she didn't answer I realized that it was a trick question. The kind you're not supposed to answer out loud.

"Where on earth did you get the idea that the polling station moved?"

This was an easy one!

"Mrs. Pellington told us that the election was canceled in all the schools!"

My father stopped pacing and faced me. He and my mother looked at each other confused. This news made them a little less angry, which meant I was not grounded for **foreverteen**—probably just forever.

"What did she say *exactly*?" my father wanted to know.

My father only asked for *exactly* things when he thought I didn't

have the facts straight. But **I DID** have the facts straight.

"She exactly said something about how there would be no more school voting ever in the world. That it would only be in local theaters," I said.

Now they looked even more confused.

So I added, "Or something like that."

"But our town doesn't have a local theater," my mom said.

"Oh yeah," I said. I forgot that every time we wanted to see a play, we had to drive all the way to Morristown. Morristown wasn't local at all.

"So if our town doesn't have a local theater, how could anyone in our town vote there?" my dad asked me.

Now **I** was **stumpified**.

"I don't know."

I **squinched** my eyes close together to try and remember exactly what Mrs. Pellington had been talking about. And just then, I felt some little memories start to drizzle in.

A big ocean wave swelled inside my belly and up to my head as **I sort of, kind of, maybe, possibly, perhaps** remembered a tiny detail that must have fallen into one of my brain creases. Which meant there was a chance that I sort of, kind of, maybe, possibly, perhaps wasn't paying the most carefulest attention to Mrs. Pellington. **I was, however, (however is a very grown-up word) paying the carefulest attention to note-passing with Elliott.** And that's when I had the big realization and looked up at my parents with the guilt of the world in my eyes.

When Elliott and I started to pay attention, I thought Mrs. Pellington was talking about voting being moved from *our* school to the local theater, but she wasn't. She was probably still telling us the story she had started about her childhood. But, because I wasn't paying attention so well, I thought that by the time I started to pay attention she must have started a new story. **I was in a worldwide canyon of trouble.**

"Do you know what kind of trouble you created for everyone?"

See what I mean? I shook my head no. That was the truth of the world. I really didn't know. Now my father started pacing again.

"Well, first of all you gave out wrong information. The voting *was* at

Chester Elementary. That's why you were on a field trip all morning. To get you out of the way for the early morning voting rush. Second of all, you had no business sitting at Mr. Sanders's desk. Third of all, you had no right to answer a phone that wasn't ringing in your own home.

There was a huge traffic jam today because all the Chester people and all the Morristown people were heading toward the Morristown polling place. By the time the Chester people finally figured out that they were supposed to vote at your school, they almost missed their chance to vote in the proper district! You might have cost Mr. Meloy the opportunity to be mayor. And he's the one you like!"

"Oh," was all I could manage to

say. The traffic jam was my fault? I felt terrible. I hadn't meant to do anything wrong at all. In fact, I meant to do the exact opposite of wrong.

"I was just trying to be an adult."

"Do you know what you're doing when you pass on information before getting the facts straight?" my mom asked.

I shook my head no. Again.

"You're starting rumors," she answered.

"Oh."

"That's a pretty kiddish thing to do, huh?"

Finally, a yes I could shake my head to.

Then my dad had a very good idea. "Let's go make dinner and we'll discuss this some more later."

I followed them into the kitchen, where they turned on the news and guess what the top story of the day was? *Mrs. Frankly B. Miller nearly ruins it for the community*. It felt terrible. I had a very heavy weight on my shoulders.

That was definitely not the way I imagined hearing about myself on the radio!

CHAPTER

My parents didn't seem to want
my help in the kitchen so I sat in the
dining room and stared at my dad's
old briefcase. I felt sad that my résumé
was still in there. It didn't even get
the chance to see any of the exciting
offices at the radio station. Come
to think of it, neither did I. Come to
think of it again, neither did anyone
in my class. **I was starting to realize
that saving the day might have actually**

ruined it. **What in the world was a person in my position supposed to do?**

Then I heard this on the radio: "*It's still unclear which way the election will go. It was a straight shot for Frank Meloy before Mrs. Frankly B. Miller steered our entire town in the wrong direction.*"

I slumped down in my chair.

For the first half of dinner, I thought maybe a miracle had occurred and my parents forgot all about the big mess of today's events. They were laughing and talking about their day and something funny that my father's assistant did. But at the part about family news, my parents put their serious faces back on.

"Do you remember that conversation we had about emergencies?" my dad asked.

I squinched my face to try and remember. Then I pressed my hands against my head so my memory would work and **va-voom**!

"Yes," I said.

"What's an emergency?"

"When there is a big accident or catastrophe. Something you tell an adult."

"Looking back, do you really think, in your heart of hearts, that there was an emergency in the radio station?"

I did not like where this was going.

"No."

"And looking back," my mother added. "Do you see how your actions affected the radio station and the entire community?"

"Yes," I said and a tear ran down

my face. My parents did not like when I cried, but even though they leaned closer and my mom even put her hand on my arm, they did not say anything comforting.

My dad fixed his face so it looked nice and professional at the same time. This was his speech face.

"I know that you want to be helpful. And we think that's a wonderful quality to have. But you need to know when you are helping and when you are creating more trouble," he said. I nodded, but he was not finished.

"I know that sometimes you think you know as much as adults."

I looked up at my dad. That sounded exactly right.

"But even adults follow the rules.

And you didn't follow the rules. When people tell you not to touch something, then everyone, adults included, respect that and they do not touch that something."

"Rules are there for a reason," my mom said. "And when you go against the rules you get yourself into trouble."

That was true, too. This was the second time in two months I got into trouble by breaking the same rule.

"For the next two nights, there will be no TV watching. Instead, we're going to let you use that time to think of a way to make things better," my dad said.

"And, no playdates with Elliott next week," my mom told me.

My eyes almost fell off my face. "Why?"

"So you'll have more time to think about what it means to break the rules," my dad said.

That night, when I was lying in bed trying to fix the entire world, more things leaked into my brain creases. When I was in the radio station and everyone was banging against the glass, they were not doing it to show excitement. They were trying to stop me. I thought they were being like umpires and telling me I was getting a home run and that Mr. Sanders was out. But they were just trying to tell me that I was saying the wrong thing to the entire planet of the world.

That's when I got out of bed and clicked my dad's briefcase open. I took out my résumé, and very carefully put it in the garbage.

RESUME
Mrs. Frankly B. Miller
Table Cleaner
Temperature Taker
Mustard Sniffer

CHAPTER

The next morning, I woke up with the worst butterflies. I had to face my entire class AND Mrs. P. I still didn't know exactly how I would make things better. But when I saw the headline of the newspaper, I felt a **machillion** percent relieved.

FRANKLY, FRANK WON, ANYWAY!

This was a very good sign. I looked at the picture of our new mayor and, **frankly**, he looked very happy. Like he just remembered it was his birthday! Everything was all fixed! What a big relief.

When I sat down for breakfast, the first thing my dad asked me was, "Do you have any ideas for how you're going to make things better?"

"But Frank Meloy won!" I said. "Everything is all fixed."

"Frank Meloy's winning doesn't erase the fact that you broke the rules."

"It doesn't?" That didn't seem fair. They just looked at me like I should know the answer.

My mother drove me to school in silence. I trudged up the stairs to my classroom feeling like I was about to take a thousandteen tests at one time.

Mrs. P. gave two long claps followed

by three short ones and we all sat down and paid attention. Elliott passed me a note.

Are you in trouble? it asked.

"Class, we need to have a very serious discussion about yesterday's antics."

Yes, I wrote back.

"We are all going to compose a letter to Mr. Sanders to apologize for what happened yesterday."

"I think Frannie should be the one to write it," Elizabeth said.

I frowned. Note-writing was one thing, but writing long letters was hard and also boring.

"We are all going to write it, but Frannie is going to come to the front of the class and lead us through it. Frannie, will you come here, please?"

I walked to the front of the class. I did not like being the center of attention when I was not saving the day.

"We want to tell Mr. Sanders the lessons we learned from yesterday. Can you tell me what those lessons are?" Mrs. P. asked. This was not a trick question.

"To keep your hands to yourself?" I answered.

"Good," Mrs. Pellington said as she wrote the answer on the board. "What else?"

"To pay attention?"

"Very good. What else?"

"Don't wander off or take matters into your own hands?"

"Excellent."

I beamed, very proud that she said

1. Keep your hands to yourself
2. Pay attention.
3. Don't wander off or take matters into your own hands.

"excellent." That's when I started to understand how to make things better. I had to show that I knew that what I did was wrong. I was going to ask Mrs. P. if I could deliver this letter to Mr. Sanders myself.

CHAPTER

The very next morning was
Saturday. At breakfast, I told my
parents what I wanted to do. Before I
knew it, my mom was on the telephone
making a **thousandteen** calls and
before I knew it again, we were in
the family car driving to the new
mayor's house. There were a lot of
photographers waiting on his lawn
and when my mom and I walked up the
path, they looked at us but didn't take

any pictures. My mother rang the bell and I started to get butterflies, and this time I also felt moths! I had to remember to tell Elliott about this fact.

A woman opened the door.

"Can I help you?" she asked us.

"Yes, I called this morning. Mrs. Frankly B. Miller would like to apologize to Mr. Meloy," my mother said to the lady. Then the lady smiled at my mom and looked at me with a wink.

"Certainly," she said. "I'll be right back." Then she shut the door and I looked at my mom and we waited and waited.

Finally, the door opened and there was the actual future mayor of Chester himself. I heard the flashes of the photographers in the background. The mayor held up his hand to them and they stopped! His hand was like a magic wand! Then he reached out his other hand to my mother and with the smallest smirk (I'm really smart about small smirks) said, "Mrs. Frankly B. Miller. I didn't think I'd ever have the pleasure."

My mom shook his hand and said, "Mr. Meloy, congratulations. My name is Anna Miller. This here," she pointed to me, "is Mrs. Frankly B. Miller." And that's when the mayor's small smirk turned into a **very big, beaming smile**.

"Well, I'll be." Then he looked at my mother and winked. "You're very young-looking to be a Mrs.," he said.

"I'm not *really* a Mrs.," I said, because I wasn't sure if he was joking. "I'm just a kid."

"Indeed, you are."

Then my mom nudged me and said,

"Don't you have something to say to Mr. Meloy, Frankly?"

"Yes. Mr. Meloy, I wanted to say that I am a millionteen sorry for any trouble I caused you. It's my whole entire fault. I'm really sorry that I almost ruined your big election."

"Well, I appreciate your apology and I accept it. Would you care to have your picture taken with me for the newspaper?"

"Yes, very, very, very much," I said. Then he took my hand and I followed him onto his front lawn.

"Ladies and gentlemen," he said to the photographers, "I'd like you to meet Mrs. Frankly B. Miller!" That's when all the photographers burst into little laughs and some people even clapped. Then there were lots and lots of flashes. The almost-mayor of Chester stooped down, put his arm around my shoulder, and smiled for a **machillion** pictures. At the very end of the pictures, I turned to him and asked him the most important question of the world.

"Mr. Meloy?"

"Yes, Frankly?"

"Can I send you my résumé?"

He laughed and patted me on the head.

"Frankly, I'd like nothing more," he said. It was the best day of my entire worldwide life.

When we got back in the car, I looked at my mom and she asked, "Ready?"

"Ready," I said. Time for stop number two.

Mr. Sanders opened his own door and seemed happier to see me than I ever would have imagined. I gave him the letter from my class and

apologized to him. And guess what!
He *also* accepted my apology!
Then he invited us inside his house for
some tea and cookies.

His house didn't have any
assistants or radio stations. And even
though it only had one office, it was
still very nice.

My mom and I sat at the kitchen
table with Mr. Sanders. He told me
that yesterday he was very upset
by what I did, but that when he
thought about it more, he realized
I was a very special kid. He said he
was very impressed that I wanted
a job. Then he told me that I
reminded him of his own self at my
age. I wasn't sure this was good
because I'm a girl and he's a boy,
but my mom told me later it was

a compliment. **I'm not so smart about compliments**.

Then Elizabeth came downstairs and we all talked and laughed. We decided that Tuesday was a very good name and that when I was eighteen, maybe I could have Tuesday's job! This was the most excited I'd been since I got my picture taken just a little while ago.

CHAPTER

When I opened my bedroom door the next morning, there was a newspaper on the other side waiting for me. On the very front page of the *Chester Times* was a picture of me hugging the mayor! I picked it up and ran downstairs. I could barely believe my own eyes. A HAPPY ENDING FOR FRANK & FRANKLY was the headline! I would never ever throw this newspaper away.

I spent that entire Sunday smiling.

I didn't think I could ever get any happier.

But I was wrong.

That night, my dad and mom came into my bedroom. My dad had something behind his back, but I couldn't see it.

"We're very proud of you," my dad said.

"Apologizing is hard to do, and you handled it just like a pro," said my mom.

"Thank you," I said.

"We thought you might like this," my dad said as he pulled out a present from behind his back and gave it to me. I opened it excitedly. And when I looked at it, I gasped the biggest gulp of air imaginable. It was a picture frame and inside the frame was the picture of me and the mayor from the newspaper. I put it on the nightstand next to my bed where I could look at it forever.

"We're very proud of you," my mom said, as she turned out my lights and closed my bedroom door almost all the way shut but not entirely. I lay in bed filled with so much **pride-itity** that I had done something that was actually grown-up.

Even though I still felt grumpy about not having a playdate with Elliott for one entire week, I felt like a real grown-up. I did all the right things. I knew I did, too, because I was going to sleep with no moths or butterflies.

But before I fell asleep, I remembered the most important thing. I got out of bed and walked over to my garbage

can. My résumé was lying at the
bottom and I pulled it out and put it
next to my bed. Tomorrow morning,
my mom said she'd take me to the
post office. I was going to put
my résumé in a professional
envelope and send it to the mayor.
He probably needed someone like me
in his office.

THE END.

About the Author

AJ Stern lives in an upside-down house in Brooklyn, NY. She has fifteen children under the age of eleven who all have very good jobs. She rides to work on a horse and only eats food that is orange. Okay, none of this is true (except the Brooklyn part), but it would be a little funny if it were. Right?

About the Illustrator

After graduating from Carnegie Mellon University, Doreen Mulryan Marts worked at Marvel Comics as a production assistant and as a product designer for Russ Berrie. Now she works as a freelance illustrator and designer from the comfort of her New Jersey home.